P9-CRS-998

COLLECTOR'S STICKER BOOK

VOLUME ONE

HOW TO USE THIS BOOK

Capture your own Bakugan using the stickers in this book! Inside you'll find lots of Bakugan warriors. Place the stickers in the appropriate spot, then fill in the information about each Bakugan—how you captured it, what kind of Ability cards to use with it, and much, much more. Use this book as a handy guide whenever you prepare to brawl.

ISBN-13: 978-0-545-12101-9   ISBN-10: 0-545-12101-9
© Spin Master Ltd/Sega Toys.
CARTOON NETWORK and the logo are trademarks of and © 2008 Cartoon Network.
BAKUGAN and BATTLE BRAWLERS, and all related titles, logos, and characters are trademarks of Spin Master LTD.
NELVANA is a trademark of Nelvana Limited. CORUS is a trademark of Corus Entertainment Inc.
Used under license by Scholastic Inc. All Rights Reserved.
Published by Scholastic Inc. SCHOLASTIC and associated logos are trademarks and/or registered trademarks of Scholastic Inc.

12 11 10 9 8 7 6 5 4 3 2 1   9 10 11 12/0
Printed in the U.S.A. First printing, March 2009

SCHOLASTIC INC.
NEW YORK   TORONTO   LONDON   AUCKLAND   SYDNEY
MEXICO CITY   NEW DELHI   HONG KONG   BUENOS AIRES

APOLLONIR

PLANETARY ATTRIBUTE:

WARRIOR CLASS: _fire_

WHEN I GOT THIS BAKUGAN: _I battled_

GATE CARDS TO USE WITH THIS BAKUGAN:

Replay

ABILITY CARDS TO USE WITH THIS BAKUGAN:

Replay

WINS: ⊙ ⊙ ⊙ ⊙ ⊙ ⊙ ⊙ ⊙ ⊙ ⊙ ⊙ ⊙ ○ ○ ○ ○ ○

LOSSES: ○ ○ ○ ○ ○ ○ ○ ○ ○ ○ ○ ○ ○ ○ ○ ○ ○

BEE STRIKER

PLANETARY ATTRIBUTE:

WARRIOR CLASS: _____

WHEN I GOT THIS BAKUGAN: _____

GATE CARDS TO USE WITH THIS BAKUGAN:

_____

_____

_____

_____

ABILITY CARDS TO USE WITH THIS BAKUGAN:

_____

_____

_____

_____

WINS: ⊛ ⊛ ⊛ ⊛ ⊛ ⊛ ⊛ ⊛ ⊛ ⊛ ◯ ◯ ◯ ◯ ◯

LOSSES: ⊛ ⊛ ⊛ ⊛ ⊛ ⊛ ⊛ ⊛ ◯ ◯ ◯ ◯ ◯ ◯ ◯

BLADE TIGRERRA

PLANETARY ATTRIBUTE:

WARRIOR CLASS: _____

WHEN I GOT THIS BAKUGAN: _____

GATE CARDS TO USE WITH THIS BAKUGAN:

_____

_____

_____

_____

ABILITY CARDS TO USE WITH THIS BAKUGAN:

_____

_____

_____

_____

WINS: ⊘ ⊘ ◎ ◎ ◎ ◎ ◎ ◎ ◎ ◎ ◎ ◎ ○ ○ ○ ○

LOSSES: ○ ○ ○ ○ ○ ○ ○ ○ ○ ○ ○ ○ ○ ○ ○ ○

CENTIPOID

PLANETARY ATTRIBUTE:

WARRIOR CLASS: _____

WHEN I GOT THIS BAKUGAN: _____

GATE CARDS TO USE WITH THIS BAKUGAN:

_____

_____

_____

_____

ABILITY CARDS TO USE WITH THIS BAKUGAN:

_____

_____

_____

_____

WINS: ⊕ ⊕ ○ ○ ○ ○ ○ ○ ○ ○ ○ ○ ○ ○ ○ ○

LOSSES: ⊕ ○ ○ ○ ○ ○ ○ ○ ○ ○ ○ ○ ○ ○ ○ ○

CLAYF

PLANETARY ATTRIBUTE:

WARRIOR CLASS: _____

WHEN I GOT THIS BAKUGAN: _____

GATE CARDS TO USE WITH THIS BAKUGAN:

_____

_____

_____

_____

ABILITY CARDS TO USE WITH THIS BAKUGAN:

_____

_____

_____

_____

WINS: ○ ○ ○ ○ ○ ○ ○ ○ ○ ○ ○ ○ ○ ○ ○

LOSSES: ○ ○ ○ ○ ○ ○ ○ ○ ○ ○ ○ ○ ○ ○ ○

CYCLOID

PLANETARY ATTRIBUTE:

WARRIOR CLASS: _____

WHEN I GOT THIS BAKUGAN: _____

GATE CARDS TO USE WITH THIS BAKUGAN:

_____

_____

_____

_____

ABILITY CARDS TO USE WITH THIS BAKUGAN:

_____

_____

_____

_____

WINS: ○ ○ ○ ○ ○ ○ ○ ○ ○ ○ ○ ○ ○ ○ ○ ○

LOSSES: ○ ○ ○ ○ ○ ○ ○ ○ ○ ○ ○ ○ ○ ○ ○ ○

DRAGONOID

PLANETARY ATTRIBUTE:

WARRIOR CLASS: _____

WHEN I GOT THIS BAKUGAN: _____

GATE CARDS TO USE WITH THIS BAKUGAN:

_____

_____

_____

_____

ABILITY CARDS TO USE WITH THIS BAKUGAN:

_____

_____

_____

_____

WINS: ⦾ ⦾ ⦾ ⦾ ⦾ ⦾ ⦾ ⦾ ⦾ ⦾ ⦾ ⦿ ⦿ ⦿ ⦿

LOSSES: ○ ○ ○ ○ ○ ○ ○ ○ ○ ○ ○ ○ ○ ○ ○

DELTA DRAGONOID

PLANETARY ATTRIBUTE:

WARRIOR CLASS: _____

WHEN I GOT THIS BAKUGAN: _____

GATE CARDS TO USE WITH THIS BAKUGAN:

_____

_____

_____

_____

ABILITY CARDS TO USE WITH THIS BAKUGAN:

_____

_____

_____

_____

WINS: ⊘ ⊘ ⊘ ⊘ ⊘ ⊘ ⊘ ⊘ ⊘ ⊘ ⊘ ⊘ ⊘ ⊘ ⊘ ⊘

LOSSES: ⊘ ⊘ ○ ○ ○ ○ ○ ○ ○ ○ ○ ○ ○ ○ ○ ○

EL CONDOR

PLANETARY ATTRIBUTE:

WARRIOR CLASS: _____

WHEN I GOT THIS BAKUGAN: _____

GATE CARDS TO USE WITH THIS BAKUGAN:

_____

_____

_____

_____

ABILITY CARDS TO USE WITH THIS BAKUGAN:

_____

_____

_____

_____

WINS: ○ ○ ○ ○ ○ ○ ○ ○ ○ ○ ○ ○ ○ ○ ○

LOSSES: ○ ○ ○ ○ ○ ○ ○ ○ ○ ○ ○ ○ ○ ○ ○

EXEDRA

PLANETARY ATTRIBUTE:

WARRIOR CLASS: _____

WHEN I GOT THIS BAKUGAN: _____

GATE CARDS TO USE WITH THIS BAKUGAN:

_____

_____

_____

_____

ABILITY CARDS TO USE WITH THIS BAKUGAN:

_____

_____

_____

_____

WINS: ⌀ ⌀ ⌀ ⌀ ⌀ ⌀ ◯ ◯ ◯ ◯ ◯ ◯ ◯ ◯ ◯ ◯ ◯

LOSSES: ◯ ◯ ◯ ◯ ◯ ◯ ◯ ◯ ◯ ◯ ◯ ◯ ◯ ◯ ◯ ◯ ◯

FALCONEER

PLANETARY ATTRIBUTE:

WARRIOR CLASS: _____

WHEN I GOT THIS BAKUGAN: _____

GATE CARDS TO USE WITH THIS BAKUGAN:

_____

_____

_____

_____

ABILITY CARDS TO USE WITH THIS BAKUGAN:

_____

_____

_____

_____

WINS: ○ ○ ○ ○ ○ ○ ○ ○ ○ ○ ○ ○ ○ ○ ○ ○ ○

LOSSES: ○ ○ ○ ○ ○ ○ ○ ○ ○ ○ ○ ○ ○ ○ ○ ○ ○ ○

FEAR RIPPER

PLANETARY ATTRIBUTE:

WARRIOR CLASS: _____

WHEN I GOT THIS BAKUGAN: _____

GATE CARDS TO USE WITH THIS BAKUGAN:

_____

_____

_____

_____

ABILITY CARDS TO USE WITH THIS BAKUGAN:

_____

_____

_____

_____

WINS: ⊘ ○ ○ ○ ○ ○ ○ ○ ○ ○ ○ ○ ○ ○ ○

LOSSES: ○ ○ ○ ○ ○ ○ ○ ○ ○ ○ ○ ○ ○ ○ ○

FOURTRESS

PLANETARY ATTRIBUTE:

WARRIOR CLASS: _____

WHEN I GOT THIS BAKUGAN: _____

GATE CARDS TO USE WITH THIS BAKUGAN:

_____

_____

_____

_____

ABILITY CARDS TO USE WITH THIS BAKUGAN:

_____

_____

_____

_____

WINS: ○ ○ ○ ○ ○ ○ ○ ○ ○ ○ ○ ○ ○ ○ ○

LOSSES: ○ ○ ○ ○ ○ ○ ○ ○ ○ ○ ○ ○ ○ ○ ○

FROSCH

PLANETARY ATTRIBUTE:

WARRIOR CLASS: _____

WHEN I GOT THIS BAKUGAN: _____

GATE CARDS TO USE WITH THIS BAKUGAN:

_____

_____

_____

_____

ABILITY CARDS TO USE WITH THIS BAKUGAN:

_____

_____

_____

_____

WINS: ○ ○ ○ ○ ○ ○ ○ ○ ○ ○ ○ ○ ○ ○ ○ ○ ○

LOSSES: ○ ○ ○ ○ ○ ○ ○ ○ ○ ○ ○ ○ ○ ○ ○ ○ ○

GARGONOID

PLANETARY ATTRIBUTE:

WARRIOR CLASS: _____

WHEN I GOT THIS BAKUGAN: _____

GATE CARDS TO USE WITH THIS BAKUGAN:

_____

_____

_____

_____

ABILITY CARDS TO USE WITH THIS BAKUGAN:

_____

_____

_____

_____

WINS: ○ ○ ○ ○ ○ ○ ○ ○ ○ ○ ○ ○ ○ ○ ○ ○

LOSSES: ○ ○ ○ ○ ○ ○ ○ ○ ○ ○ ○ ○ ○ ○ ○ ○ ○

GOREM

PLANETARY ATTRIBUTE:

WARRIOR CLASS: _____

WHEN I GOT THIS BAKUGAN: _____

GATE CARDS TO USE WITH THIS BAKUGAN:

_____

_____

_____

_____

ABILITY CARDS TO USE WITH THIS BAKUGAN:

_____

_____

_____

_____

WINS: ○ ○ ○ ○ ○ ○ ○ ○ ○ ○ ○ ○ ○ ○ ○

LOSSES: ○ ○ ○ ○ ○ ○ ○ ○ ○ ○ ○ ○ ○ ○ ○

GRIFFON

PLANETARY ATTRIBUTE:

WARRIOR CLASS: _____

WHEN I GOT THIS BAKUGAN: _____

GATE CARDS TO USE WITH THIS BAKUGAN:

_____

_____

_____

_____

ABILITY CARDS TO USE WITH THIS BAKUGAN:

_____

_____

_____

_____

WINS: ○ ○ ○ ○ ○ ○ ○ ○ ○ ○ ○ ○ ○ ○ ○ ○

LOSSES: ○ ○ ○ ○ ○ ○ ○ ○ ○ ○ ○ ○ ○ ○ ○ ○

HAMMER GOREM

PLANETARY ATTRIBUTE:

WARRIOR CLASS: _____

WHEN I GOT THIS BAKUGAN: _____

GATE CARDS TO USE WITH THIS BAKUGAN:

_____

_____

_____

_____

ABILITY CARDS TO USE WITH THIS BAKUGAN:

_____

_____

_____

_____

WINS: ○○○○○○○○○○○○○○○○○○

LOSSES: ○○○○○○○○○○○○○○○○○○

HARPUS

PLANETARY ATTRIBUTE:

WARRIOR CLASS: _____

WHEN I GOT THIS BAKUGAN: _____

GATE CARDS TO USE WITH THIS BAKUGAN:

_____

_____

_____

_____

ABILITY CARDS TO USE WITH THIS BAKUGAN:

_____

_____

_____

_____

WINS: ◯ ◯ ◯ ◯ ◯ ◯ ◯ ◯ ◯ ◯ ◯ ◯ ◯ ◯ ◯

LOSSES: ◯ ◯ ◯ ◯ ◯ ◯ ◯ ◯ ◯ ◯ ◯ ◯ ◯ ◯ ◯

HYDRANOID

PLANETARY ATTRIBUTE:

WARRIOR CLASS: _____

WHEN I GOT THIS BAKUGAN: _____

GATE CARDS TO USE WITH THIS BAKUGAN:

_____

_____

_____

_____

ABILITY CARDS TO USE WITH THIS BAKUGAN:

_____

_____

_____

_____

WINS: ○ ○ ○ ○ ○ ○ ○ ○ ○ ○ ○ ○ ○ ○ ○ ○ ○ ○ ○

LOSSES: ○ ○ ○ ○ ○ ○ ○ ○ ○ ○ ○ ○ ○ ○ ○ ○ ○ ○ ○

HYNOID

PLANETARY ATTRIBUTE:

WARRIOR CLASS: _____

WHEN I GOT THIS BAKUGAN: _____

GATE CARDS TO USE WITH THIS BAKUGAN:

_____

_____

_____

_____

ABILITY CARDS TO USE WITH THIS BAKUGAN:

_____

_____

_____

_____

WINS: ○ ○ ○ ○ ○ ○ ○ ○ ○ ○ ○ ○ ○ ○ ○

LOSSES: ○ ○ ○ ○ ○ ○ ○ ○ ○ ○ ○ ○ ○ ○ ○

JUGGERNOID

PLANETARY ATTRIBUTE:

WARRIOR CLASS: _____

WHEN I GOT THIS BAKUGAN: _____

GATE CARDS TO USE WITH THIS BAKUGAN:

_____

_____

_____

_____

ABILITY CARDS TO USE WITH THIS BAKUGAN:

_____

_____

_____

_____

WINS: ○ ○ ○ ○ ○ ○ ○ ○ ○ ○ ○ ○ ○ ○

LOSSES: ○ ○ ○ ○ ○ ○ ○ ○ ○ ○ ○ ○ ○ ○

LASERMAN

PLANETARY ATTRIBUTE:

WARRIOR CLASS: _____

WHEN I GOT THIS BAKUGAN: _____

GATE CARDS TO USE WITH THIS BAKUGAN:

_____

_____

_____

_____

ABILITY CARDS TO USE WITH THIS BAKUGAN:

_____

_____

_____

_____

WINS: ○ ○ ○ ○ ○ ○ ○ ○ ○ ○ ○ ○ ○ ○ ○ ○ ○

LOSSES: ○ ○ ○ ○ ○ ○ ○ ○ ○ ○ ○ ○ ○ ○ ○ ○ ○

LIMULUS

PLANETARY ATTRIBUTE:

WARRIOR CLASS: _____

WHEN I GOT THIS BAKUGAN: _____

GATE CARDS TO USE WITH THIS BAKUGAN:

_____

_____

_____

_____

ABILITY CARDS TO USE WITH THIS BAKUGAN:

_____

_____

_____

_____

WINS: ○ ○ ○ ○ ○ ○ ○ ○ ○ ○ ○ ○ ○ ○ ○ ○

LOSSES: ○ ○ ○ ○ ○ ○ ○ ○ ○ ○ ○ ○ ○ ○ ○ ○ ○

MANION

PLANETARY ATTRIBUTE:

WARRIOR CLASS: _____

WHEN I GOT THIS BAKUGAN: _____

GATE CARDS TO USE WITH THIS BAKUGAN:

_____

_____

_____

_____

ABILITY CARDS TO USE WITH THIS BAKUGAN:

_____

_____

_____

WINS: ○ ○ ○ ○ ○ ○ ○ ○ ○ ○ ○ ○ ○ ○ ○ ○ ○

LOSSES: ○ ○ ○ ○ ○ ○ ○ ○ ○ ○ ○ ○ ○ ○ ○ ○ ○

MANTRIS

PLANETARY ATTRIBUTE:

WARRIOR CLASS: _____

WHEN I GOT THIS BAKUGAN: _____

GATE CARDS TO USE WITH THIS BAKUGAN:

_____

_____

_____

_____

ABILITY CARDS TO USE WITH THIS BAKUGAN:

_____

_____

_____

_____

WINS: ○ ○ ○ ○ ○ ○ ○ ○ ○ ○ ○ ○ ○ ○

LOSSES: ○ ○ ○ ○ ○ ○ ○ ○ ○ ○ ○ ○ ○ ○

MONARUS

PLANETARY ATTRIBUTE:

WARRIOR CLASS: _____

WHEN I GOT THIS BAKUGAN: _____

GATE CARDS TO USE WITH THIS BAKUGAN:

_____

_____

_____

_____

ABILITY CARDS TO USE WITH THIS BAKUGAN:

_____

_____

_____

_____

WINS: ◯◯◯◯◯◯◯◯◯◯◯◯◯◯◯◯

LOSSES: ◯◯◯◯◯◯◯◯◯◯◯◯◯◯◯◯

OBERUS

PLANETARY ATTRIBUTE:

WARRIOR CLASS: _____

WHEN I GOT THIS BAKUGAN: _____

GATE CARDS TO USE WITH THIS BAKUGAN:

_____

_____

_____

_____

ABILITY CARDS TO USE WITH THIS BAKUGAN:

_____

_____

_____

_____

WINS: ○ ○ ○ ○ ○ ○ ○ ○ ○ ○ ○ ○ ○ ○ ○ ○ ○ ○

LOSSES: ○ ○ ○ ○ ○ ○ ○ ○ ○ ○ ○ ○ ○ ○ ○ ○ ○ ○

PREYAS

PLANETARY ATTRIBUTE:

WARRIOR CLASS: _____

WHEN I GOT THIS BAKUGAN: _____

GATE CARDS TO USE WITH THIS BAKUGAN:

_____
_____
_____
_____

ABILITY CARDS TO USE WITH THIS BAKUGAN:

_____
_____
_____
_____

WINS: ○ ○ ○ ○ ○ ○ ○ ○ ○ ○ ○ ○ ○ ○ ○ ○ ○

LOSSES: ○ ○ ○ ○ ○ ○ ○ ○ ○ ○ ○ ○ ○ ○ ○ ○ ○

RATTLEOID

PLANETARY ATTRIBUTE:

WARRIOR CLASS: _____

WHEN I GOT THIS BAKUGAN: _____

GATE CARDS TO USE WITH THIS BAKUGAN:

_____

_____

_____

_____

ABILITY CARDS TO USE WITH THIS BAKUGAN:

_____

_____

_____

_____

W ○ ○ ○ ○ ○ ○ ○ ○ ○ ○ ○ ○ ○ ○ ○ ○ ○

LOSSES: ○ ○ ○ ○ ○ ○ ○ ○ ○ ○ ○ ○ ○ ○ ○ ○

RAVENOID

PLANETARY ATTRIBUTE:

WARRIOR CLASS: _____

WHEN I GOT THIS BAKUGAN: _____

GATE CARDS TO USE WITH THIS BAKUGAN:

_____

_____

_____

_____

ABILITY CARDS TO USE WITH THIS BAKUGAN:

_____

_____

_____

_____

WINS: ○ ○ ○ ○ ○ ○ ○ ○ ○ ○ ○ ○ ○ ○ ○ ○

LOSSES: ○ ○ ○ ○ ○ ○ ○ ○ ○ ○ ○ ○ ○ ○ ○ ○

REAPER

PLANETARY ATTRIBUTE:

WARRIOR CLASS: _____

WHEN I GOT THIS BAKUGAN: _____

GATE CARDS TO USE WITH THIS BAKUGAN:

_____

_____

_____

_____

ABILITY CARDS TO USE WITH THIS BAKUGAN:

_____

_____

_____

_____

WINS: ○ ○ ○ ○ ○ ○ ○ ○ ○ ○ ○ ○ ○ ○ ○

LOSSES: ○ ○ ○ ○ ○ ○ ○ ○ ○ ○ ○ ○ ○ ○ ○

ROBOTALLIAN

PLANETARY ATTRIBUTE:

WARRIOR CLASS: _____

WHEN I GOT THIS BAKUGAN: _____

GATE CARDS TO USE WITH THIS BAKUGAN:

_____

_____

_____

_____

ABILITY CARDS TO USE WITH THIS BAKUGAN:

_____

_____

_____

_____

WINS: ○ ○ ○ ○ ○ ○ ○ ○ ○ ○ ○ ○ ○ ○ ○ ○

LOSSES: ○ ○ ○ ○ ○ ○ ○ ○ ○ ○ ○ ○ ○ ○ ○ ○

SAURUS

PLANETARY ATTRIBUTE:

WARRIOR CLASS: _____

WHEN I GOT THIS BAKUGAN: _____

GATE CARDS TO USE WITH THIS BAKUGAN:

_____

_____

_____

ABILITY CARDS TO USE WITH THIS BAKUGAN:

_____

_____

_____

WINS: ○ ○ ○ ○ ○ ○ ○ ○ ○ ○ ○ ○ ○ ○ ○ ○ ○ ○

LOSSES: ○ ○ ○ ○ ○ ○ ○ ○ ○ ○ ○ ○ ○ ○ ○ ○ ○

SERPENOID

PLANETARY ATTRIBUTE:

WARRIOR CLASS: _____

WHEN I GOT THIS BAKUGAN: _____

GATE CARDS TO USE WITH THIS BAKUGAN:

_____

_____

_____

_____

ABILITY CARDS TO USE WITH THIS BAKUGAN:

_____

_____

_____

_____

WINS: ○ ○ ○ ○ ○ ○ ○ ○ ○ ○ ○ ○ ○ ○ ○

LOSSES: ○ ○ ○ ○ ○ ○ ○ ○ ○ ○ ○ ○ ○ ○ ○

SIEGE

PLANETARY ATTRIBUTE:

WARRIOR CLASS: _____

WHEN I GOT THIS BAKUGAN: _____

GATE CARDS TO USE WITH THIS BAKUGAN:

_____

_____

_____

_____

ABILITY CARDS TO USE WITH THIS BAKUGAN:

_____

_____

_____

_____

WINS: ○ ○ ○ ○ ○ ○ ○ ○ ○ ○ ○ ○ ○ ○ ○

LOSSES: ○ ○ ○ ○ ○ ○ ○ ○ ○ ○ ○ ○ ○ ○ ○

SIRENOID

PLANETARY ATTRIBUTE:

WARRIOR CLASS: _____

WHEN I GOT THIS BAKUGAN: _____

GATE CARDS TO USE WITH THIS BAKUGAN:

_____

_____

_____

_____

ABILITY CARDS TO USE WITH THIS BAKUGAN:

_____

_____

_____

_____

WINS: ○ ○ ○ ○ ○ ○ ○ ○ ○ ○ ○ ○ ○ ○ ○ ○

LOSSES: ○ ○ ○ ○ ○ ○ ○ ○ ○ ○ ○ ○ ○ ○ ○ ○

SKYRESS

PLANETARY ATTRIBUTE:

WARRIOR CLASS: _____

WHEN I GOT THIS BAKUGAN: _____

GATE CARDS TO USE WITH THIS BAKUGAN:

_____

_____

_____

_____

ABILITY CARDS TO USE WITH THIS BAKUGAN:

_____

_____

_____

_____

WINS: ⬤ ○ ○ ○ ○ ○ ○ ○ ○ ○ ○ ○ ○ ○ ○ ○ ○ ○

LOSSES: ○ ○ ○ ○ ○ ○ ○ ○ ○ ○ ○ ○ ○ ○ ○ ○ ○ ○

STINGSLASH

PLANETARY ATTRIBUTE:

WARRIOR CLASS: _____

WHEN I GOT THIS BAKUGAN: _____

GATE CARDS TO USE WITH THIS BAKUGAN:

_____

_____

_____

_____

ABILITY CARDS TO USE WITH THIS BAKUGAN:

_____

_____

_____

_____

WINS: ○ ○ ○ ○ ○ ○ ○ ○ ○ ○ ○ ○ ○ ○ ○ ○ ○

LOSSES: ○ ○ ○ ○ ○ ○ ○ ○ ○ ○ ○ ○ ○ ○ ○ ○ ○

STORM SKYRESS

PLANETARY ATTRIBUTE:

WARRIOR CLASS: _____

WHEN I GOT THIS BAKUGAN: _____

GATE CARDS TO USE WITH THIS BAKUGAN:

_____

_____

_____

_____

ABILITY CARDS TO USE WITH THIS BAKUGAN:

_____

_____

_____

WINS: ○ ○ ○ ○ ○ ○ ○ ○ ○ ○ ○ ○ ○ ○ ○ ○ ○ ○

LOSSES: ○ ○ ○ ○ ○ ○ ○ ○ ○ ○ ○ ○ ○ ○ ○ ○ ○ ○

TENTACLEAR

PLANETARY ATTRIBUTE:

WARRIOR CLASS: _____

WHEN I GOT THIS BAKUGAN: _____

GATE CARDS TO USE WITH THIS BAKUGAN:

_____

_____

_____

_____

ABILITY CARDS TO USE WITH THIS BAKUGAN:

_____

_____

_____

_____

WINS: ○ ○ ○ ○ ○ ○ ○ ○ ○ ○ ○ ○ ○ ○ ○ ○

LOSSES: ○ ○ ○ ○ ○ ○ ○ ○ ○ ○ ○ ○ ○ ○ ○ ○

TERRORCLAW

PLANETARY ATTRIBUTE:

WARRIOR CLASS: _____

WHEN I GOT THIS BAKUGAN: _____

GATE CARDS TO USE WITH THIS BAKUGAN:

_____

_____

_____

_____

ABILITY CARDS TO USE WITH THIS BAKUGAN:

_____

_____

_____

_____

WINS: ○ ○ ○ ○ ○ ○ ○ ○ ○ ○ ○ ○ ○ ○ ○ ○ ○

LOSSES: ○ ○ ○ ○ ○ ○ ○ ○ ○ ○ ○ ○ ○ ○ ○ ○ ○

TIGRERRA

PLANETARY ATTRIBUTE:

WARRIOR CLASS: _____

WHEN I GOT THIS BAKUGAN: _____

GATE CARDS TO USE WITH THIS BAKUGAN:

_____

_____

_____

_____

ABILITY CARDS TO USE WITH THIS BAKUGAN:

_____

_____

_____

_____

WINS: ○ ○ ○ ○ ○ ○ ○ ○ ○ ○ ○ ○ ○ ○ ○

LOSSES: ○ ○ ○ ○ ○ ○ ○ ○ ○ ○ ○ ○ ○ ○ ○

TUSKOR

PLANETARY ATTRIBUTE:

WARRIOR CLASS: _____

WHEN I GOT THIS BAKUGAN: _____

GATE CARDS TO USE WITH THIS BAKUGAN:

_____

_____

_____

_____

ABILITY CARDS TO USE WITH THIS BAKUGAN:

_____

_____

_____

_____

WINS: ○ ○ ○ ○ ○ ○ ○ ○ ○ ○ ○ ○ ○ ○ ○

LOSSES: ○ ○ ○ ○ ○ ○ ○ ○ ○ ○ ○ ○ ○ ○ ○ ○

WARIUS

PLANETARY ATTRIBUTE:

WARRIOR CLASS: _____

WHEN I GOT THIS BAKUGAN: _____

GATE CARDS TO USE WITH THIS BAKUGAN:

_____

_____

_____

_____

ABILITY CARDS TO USE WITH THIS BAKUGAN:

_____

_____

_____

_____

WINS: ○ ○ ○ ○ ○ ○ ○ ○ ○ ○ ○ ○ ○ ○ ○

LOSSES: ○ ○ ○ ○ ○ ○ ○ ○ ○ ○ ○ ○ ○ ○ ○

WAVERN

PLANETARY ATTRIBUTE:

WARRIOR CLASS: _____

WHEN I GOT THIS BAKUGAN: _____

GATE CARDS TO USE WITH THIS BAKUGAN:

_____

_____

_____

_____

ABILITY CARDS TO USE WITH THIS BAKUGAN:

_____

_____

_____

_____

WINS: ○ ○ ○ ○ ○ ○ ○ ○ ○ ○ ○ ○ ○ ○ ○

LOSSES: ○ ○ ○ ○ ○ ○ ○ ○ ○ ○ ○ ○ ○ ○ ○

WORMQUAKE

PLANETARY ATTRIBUTE:

WARRIOR CLASS: _____

WHEN I GOT THIS BAKUGAN: _____

GATE CARDS TO USE WITH THIS BAKUGAN:

_____

_____

_____

_____

ABILITY CARDS TO USE WITH THIS BAKUGAN:

_____

_____

_____

_____

WINS: ○ ○ ○ ○ ○ ○ ○ ○ ○ ○ ○ ○ ○ ○ ○

LOSSES: ○ ○ ○ ○ ○ ○ ○ ○ ○ ○ ○ ○ ○ ○ ○